D0493696
The Little Forest
Elf Oak Wood
Gaston's Cave
Elf Windmill
Little Castle
The Meadow
Great Elf Tree
Elf Farm
Mrs Witch's House
Royal Golf Course
Frog Pond
N
W
E
S
The Bramble Woods
The Pine Forest

Published by Ladybird Books Ltd 2011
A Penguin Company
Penguin Books Ltd, 80 Strand, London, WC2R 0RL, UK
Penguin Books Australia Ltd, Camberwell, Victoria, Australia
Penguin Books (NZ), 67 Apollo Drive, Rosedale, Auckland
0632, New Zealand (a divison of Pearson New Zealand Ltd)

www.ladybird.com

ISBN 978-1-40930-926-0
001 - 10 9 8 7 6 5 4 3 2 1

Printed in China

This book is based on the TV Series 'Ben and Holly's Little Kingdom'
'Ben and Holly's Little Kingdom' is created by Neville Astley and Mark Baker

www.littlekingdom.co.uk

The Magical Tale of Ben and Holly's Little Kingdom

Royal Fairy Family Tree

Elf Family Tree

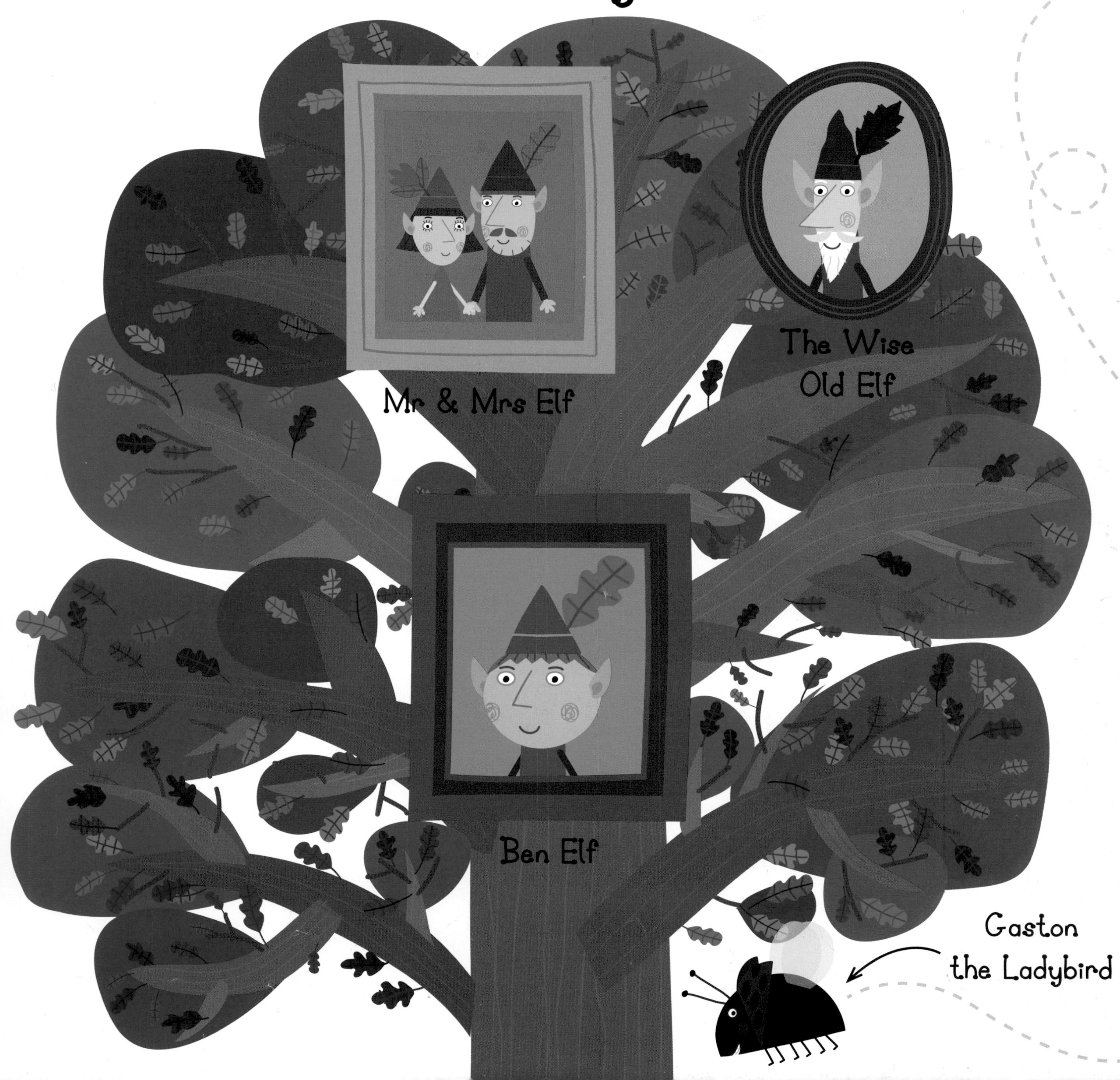

Once upon a time, hidden behind thorny brambles, there was a land of elves and fairies called the Little Kingdom.

Everyone who lived here
was very, very small.

Holly was a fairy princess and she lived with her mummy and daddy in a tiny castle called the Little Castle.

Being a fairy, Holly had wings and a magic wand.

Hi, I'm Holly.

But being a young fairy,
Holly was still learning how
to fly and do magic spells.

Ooh, what happened?

Oops!

Oh no, why isn't it working?

Eek!

Very often her spells didn't work out quite as she expected.

Holly's best friend was Ben Elf.

Ben lived on the other side of the Little Kingdom in a hollowed out oak tree called the Great Elf Tree.

In fact all the elves lived in the Great Elf Tree. It was like a sort of apartment block.

I'm an elf! Tooooot!!

Hello, Ben.
Squeak!

Being an elf, Ben didn't do magic and he didn't have wings. But he was very good at

running,

jumping,

climbing
and making things,
especially toys.

Ben and Holly's special friend was Gaston the Ladybird. Gaston lived in a smelly cave and was a little bit like a dog.

He liked to bark.

He liked to fetch sticks.

He liked to eat smelly food.

He liked to roll on his back and have his tummy tickled.

Ben standing
on a carrot.
Holly with
a tomato.

Remember what we said about everyone who lived in the Little Kingdom being very, very small?

Well, they really were small.

But that didn't stop Ben and Holly from having BIG adventures.

One day, Holly's mummy and daddy, King and Queen Thistle, decided it was time for Holly to have some proper magic lessons.

They sent out word that they were looking for a magic nanny. A few fairies applied for the job, but only one was just right, and she was called Nanny Plum.

Nanny Plum taught Holly and the other fairy children how to do spells.

Abraca Zobbedy!

Zig zag zig! Make it big!

But sometimes even Nanny Plum's spells went a bit wrong.

Eugh! What's that snail doing here?

Birdy windy!

Aaaaaaah!
Croak! Croak!

Ben was taught by a wise old elf who was called the Wise Old Elf.

He was wise.

He was old.

And he was an elf!

Ahem! No flying or magic please!

Elves, and in particular the Wise Old Elf, really didn't approve of magic.

Although Nanny Plum and the Wise Old Elf disagreed about **a lot** of things, especially when they taught the children, deep down they were friends.

Ho ho ho

Ha ha ha

Sometimes, Nanny Plum
needed non-magic help
from the elves . . .

and sometimes, the Wise Old Elf
needed some magic help from
the fairies.

Fairies and elves were often friends in the Little Kingdom. And Ben and Holly were the best of friends.

At the end of each day, Ben and Holly would say goodnight to each other and go back to their homes.

Safely tucked in bed, Holly would tell her daddy about the spells she learnt. Then King Thistle would read her a story.

Cosy in his bed, Ben would tell his mummy about the things he made that day. Then Mrs Elf would read him a story.

And warm and sleepy in his basket, Gaston would fall asleep in his lovely, messy, smelly cave, which just happened to be right in the middle of the Little Kingdom.

Zzzzzzz

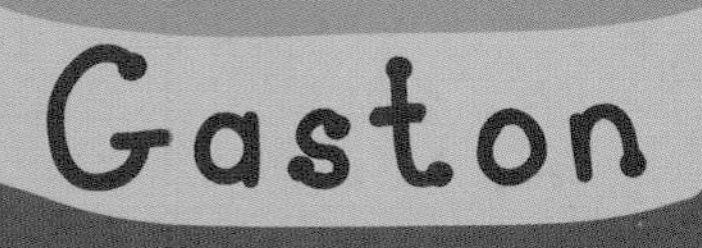

The End